BIGGEST NAMES IN SPORTS

# ANTHONY DAVIS

## BASKETBALL STAR

by Greg Bates

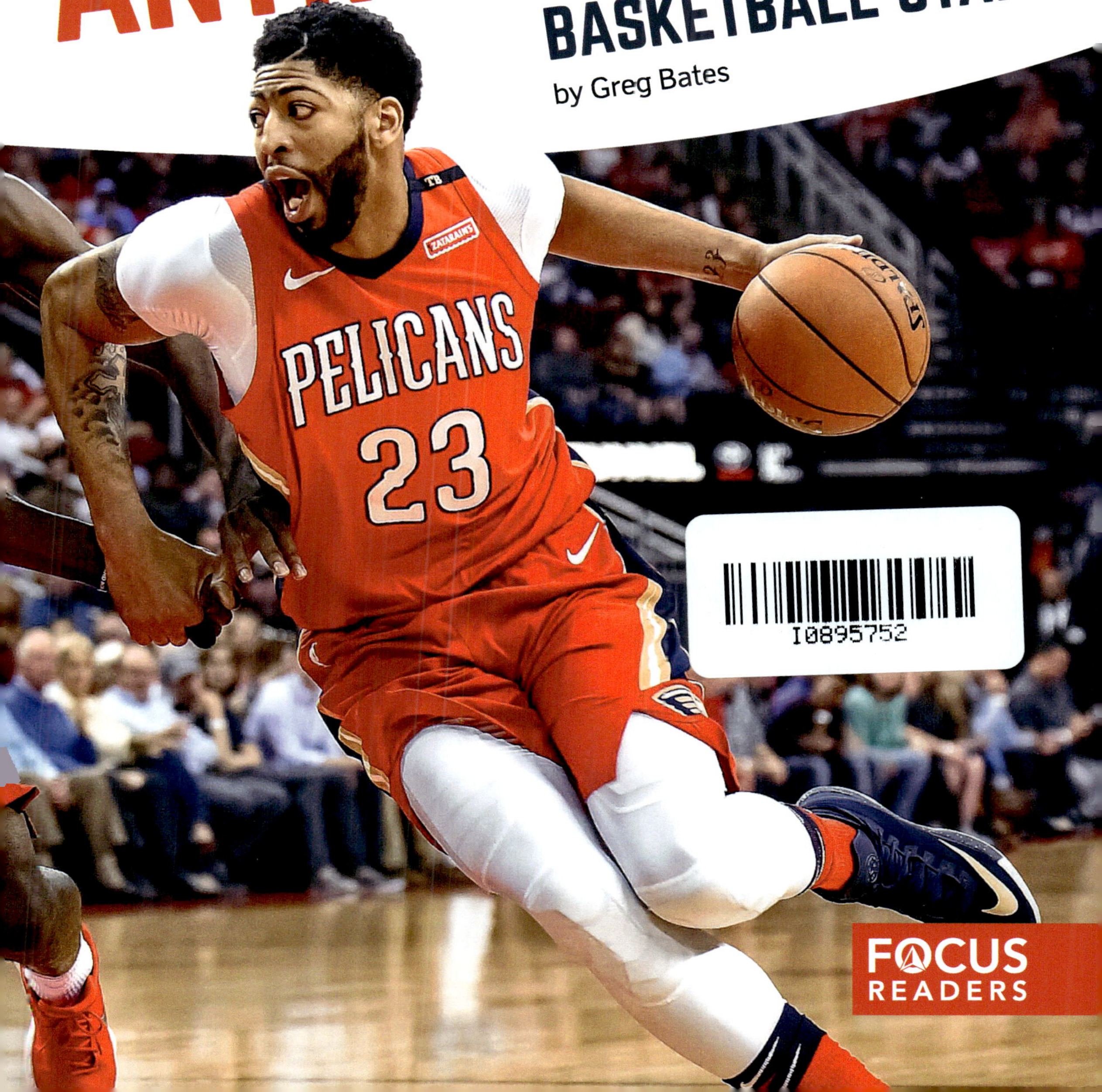




FOCUS READERS

WWW.FOCUSREADERS.COM



Focus Readers is distributed by North Star Editions:
sales@northstareditions.com | 888-417-0195

Produced for Focus Readers by Red Line Editorial.

Photographs ©: Eric Christian Smith/AP Images, cover, 1; Scott Threlkeld/AP Images, 4–5, 7, 9, 22–23; Damen Jackson/Cal Sports Media/AP Images, 10–11, 12; David J. Phillip/AP Images, 15; Bill Kostroun/AP Images, 16–17; Kathy Willens/AP Images, 19; Kyle Terada/AP Images, 21; Marcio Jose Sanchez/AP Images, 25; Mark J. Terrill/AP Images, 27; Red Line Editorial, 29

**Library of Congress Cataloging-in-Publication Data**
Library of Congress Cataloging-in-Publication Data is available on the Library of Congress website.

**ISBN**
978-1-64185-318-7 (hardcover)
978-1-64185-376-7 (paperback)
978-1-64185-492-4 (ebook pdf)
978-1-64185-434-4 (hosted ebook)

Printed in the United States of America
Mankato, MN
October, 2018

## ABOUT THE AUTHOR

Greg Bates is a freelance sports journalist based in Green Bay, Wisconsin. He has covered the Green Bay Packers for a decade. He has written for outlets such as *USA Today Sports Weekly*, the Associated Press, Green Bay Packers Yearbook, and USA Hockey. Greg and his wife have a young daughter.

# TABLE OF CONTENTS

BLOCKS
PIERRE'S PALS
PELICANS
23
PELICANS
3
SMOOTHIE KING
TISSOT
PLAYOFFS

## CHAPTER 1

# PLAYOFF DOMINANCE

The shot went up, but it didn't go in. That's when Anthony Davis's eyes got big. He knew exactly what to do. It's what he's best at. The New Orleans Pelicans star went to the rim. With such long arms, Davis barely had to jump. He grabbed the ball in midair. In an instant, he threw down a monster slam dunk.

**Davis dunks over a Portland defender during a 2018 playoff game.**

The home crowd erupted. The players on the Pelicans' bench could hardly contain their excitement. As Davis ran down the court, he sported a huge grin on his face. It was a critical moment in the game. The Pelicans were battling the

## FEAR THE BROW

**Some people know about Anthony Davis because of his incredible basketball skills. Others know him because of his unibrow. That means his two eyebrows meet in the middle to form one long eyebrow. The unibrow is something Davis didn't always like. But he started to love it over time. There isn't another player in the league with that specific look. Davis even trademarked the phrase "Fear the Brow."**

Davis pumps up the crowd after draining a three-pointer against the Trail Blazers.

Portland Trail Blazers in the first round of the 2018 playoffs.

Davis had a lot to be happy about that night. Every shot he took seemed to go in. He went up for a jump shot. It was good.

He got inside for an easy layup. That was good, too. Next was another slam dunk. For good measure, Davis stepped outside and drained a three-pointer. Whatever Davis did, it was perfect.

Davis **dominated** in the biggest game of his young career. The Pelicans ended up beating the Blazers 131–123. That victory gave the Pelicans a series **sweep**. It meant Davis would move on to the second round of the playoffs for the first time in his career.

Davis scored a team-record 47 points in that series-clinching game. In fact, he has always played well in big games. But this performance was different. It was in

Davis blocks a shot by Trail Blazers guard Wade Baldwin IV during a 2018 playoff game.

the playoffs. Davis showed that he was one of the best players in the National Basketball Association (NBA).

JRW
Reebok
32

CHAPTER 2

# A BUDDING YOUNG STAR

Anthony Davis was born in Chicago, Illinois, on March 11, 1993. He grew up playing basketball, and he was always a great shooter. But as an eighth-grader, Anthony was just 5 feet 9 inches (175 cm) tall. Then he hit a **growth spurt**. By his sophomore year of high school, he was 6 feet 2 inches (188 cm) tall.

**Anthony Davis prepares to shoot during a 2011 all-star game for high school players.**

An 18-year-old Anthony Davis goes up for a dunk during a high school all-star game.

Anthony went to Perspectives Charter School on the South Side of Chicago. He played varsity basketball there for four seasons. Anthony was a shooting guard. He was known for hitting three-pointers.

As a senior, Anthony hit another growth spurt. He shot up to 6 feet 10 inches (208 cm) tall. He towered over most of the players he competed against. During his senior year, Anthony was dominant.

## A SKILLED BIG MAN

During one period of time in high school, Anthony Davis grew 8 inches (20 cm) in just 18 months. He felt lucky that he didn't have any knee pains. It's not normal for kids to grow that quickly in such a short amount of time. Davis was fortunate. He already had great basketball skills, and now he had height. He could do things most big players couldn't. He could shoot from the outside. He could also shoot well close to the basket.

He averaged 32 points, 22 rebounds, and 7 blocked shots per game.

College coaches took notice of these big numbers. Most of the top basketball programs went after him. Anthony ended up choosing to play for the University of Kentucky.

As a freshman at Kentucky, Anthony Davis was nearly unstoppable. So was his team. Davis averaged 14.2 points, 10.4 rebounds, and 4.7 blocks per game.

The Kentucky Wildcats had an amazing group of players that year. The team went into the NCAA Tournament as the favorites to win the national title. And they did exactly that by beating the

Davis takes it to the hole during the 2012 NCAA championship game.

Kansas Jayhawks in the final. It was Kentucky's eighth national championship. Davis was only the fourth freshman ever named the Most Outstanding Player of the Final Four.

25

## CHAPTER 3

# AN IMMEDIATE IMPACT

After a great season at Kentucky, Davis decided to enter the 2012 NBA Draft. The New Orleans Hornets selected him with the No. 1 overall pick. On draft day, Davis was all smiles. He gave his mom a big hug before he went to the stage to shake the hand of NBA commissioner David Stern.

**Davis shakes hands with the NBA commissioner after becoming the No. 1 overall pick in 2012.**

Being the top pick in the draft brings high **expectations**. Davis was now the face of the **franchise**. It didn't take him long to make an impact in the NBA. He averaged 13.5 points, 8.2 rebounds, and 1.8 blocks per game. He placed second in the NBA Rookie of the Year voting. Remarkably, Davis was still only a teenager. He was young, with plenty to learn about basketball. But he was clearly a talented player.

The next year, the Hornets changed their name to the Pelicans. And after a solid first season, Davis continued to improve. He played so well in his second year he was named to the **All-Star** team.

Davis drives to the basket during his second NBA season.

It was a great honor, but Davis wasn't satisfied. He wanted to help his team reach the playoffs.

That's exactly what happened the following year. Davis had his best season yet. Best of all, the Pelicans made the playoffs. Unfortunately, they were no match for the Golden State Warriors. New Orleans lost all four of its playoff games that year. But Davis and his teammates

## REPRESENTING HIS COUNTRY

**Davis has represented the United States several times over the years. At age 19, he was chosen to be a member of the 2012 US Olympic Men's Basketball Team. He was the youngest player on the squad. Davis helped Team USA go undefeated and win the gold medal. Two years later, Davis played on the 2014 USA World Cup Team. Once again, Team USA came out on top.**

Davis shoots over a Warriors defender during a 2015 playoff game.

weren't discouraged. They were eager to get back to the postseason.

NBA
SPALDING
PELICANS
23
SPALDING
TANS
2
LAUVERGNE
77
MURRA
5

CHAPTER 4

# A FABULOUS SIXTH SEASON

Anthony Davis played great in the first five seasons of his career. But in his sixth year, he took things to another level. Davis finished second in the NBA in scoring during the 2017–18 season. Only James Harden of the Houston Rockets averaged more points. Davis also averaged 11.1 rebounds per game.

**Davis throws down a spectacular dunk against the San Antonio Spurs in 2018.**

He was one of only 11 players to average a **double-double** in points and rebounds.

Davis enjoys his individual success. But he enjoys it more when his team is playing its best. And New Orleans did well in Davis's sixth season. The Pelicans advanced to the second round of the playoffs for the first time in years. But once again, the Golden State Warriors proved to be too much. They beat the Pelicans four games to one.

Despite the playoff loss, Davis had a lot to be proud of. He was named a Most Valuable Player (MVP) finalist. James Harden and Cleveland Cavaliers superstar LeBron James were also finalists. Davis

Davis tries to dribble past Warriors star Steph Curry during a 2018 playoff game.

didn't win the award, but he showed NBA fans what a great player he is.

Davis was also a finalist for Defensive Player of the Year. He was the only player in the NBA to be a top-three finalist for multiple individual postseason awards.

After starting out as a short guard in high school, Davis has transformed

## GIVING BACK

**Davis is very active in the New Orleans community. In fact, he has received the NBA Cares Community Assist Award twice. It recognized him for his charitable efforts in New Orleans. Davis also started AD's Flight Academy. The program helps people of all ages. Every month, the program does something for the community. For example, it has held holiday shopping sprees and provided meals for the homeless.**

Davis shows a Los Angeles crowd why he's one of the most exciting players in the NBA.

into a great power forward. In fact, he's one of the best big men in the NBA. And Pelicans fans expect that Davis will only get better.

# ANTHONY DAVIS

- Height: 6 feet 10 inches (208 cm)
- Weight: 253 pounds (115 kg)
- Birth date: March 11, 1993
- Birthplace: Chicago, Illinois
- High school: Perspectives Charter School (Chicago, Illinois)
- College: University of Kentucky (Lexington, Kentucky) (2011–12)
- NBA team: New Orleans Hornets/Pelicans (2012–)
- Major awards: NCAA national champion (2012); NBA All-Star Game Most Valuable Player (2017)

Chicago
Lexington
New Orleans

## FOCUS ON
# ANTHONY DAVIS

*Write your answers on a separate piece of paper.*

1. Write a sentence that describes the main idea of Chapter 1.
2. If Davis had not hit a growth spurt in high school, do you think he would have ended up in the NBA? Why or why not?
3. Which team did the Pelicans sweep in the 2018 playoffs?
   - A. Portland Trail Blazers
   - B. Golden State Warriors
   - C. Cleveland Cavaliers
4. Why didn't Davis stay at Kentucky after his freshman year?
   - A. because he wanted to play for a different college
   - B. because he was good enough to play in the NBA
   - C. because the coach didn't want him on the team

*Answer key on page 32.*

# GLOSSARY

**All-Star**
Having to do with the best players in a league.

**charitable**
Having to do with people who help others by giving money or time.

**dominated**
Showed that one player was clearly better than an opponent.

**double-double**
A game in which a player has double-digit numbers in two categories.

**expectations**
Strong beliefs that a person will do something.

**franchise**
A sports team.

**growth spurt**
When a person becomes much taller in a short amount of time.

**sweep**
Winning all the games in a series.

# TO LEARN MORE

## BOOKS


DeMocker, Michael. *Anthony Davis*. Kennett Square, PA: Purple Toad Publishing, 2018.

Fishman, Jon M. *Anthony Davis*. Minneapolis: Lerner Publications, 2016.

Glave, Tom. *Anthony Davis*. Minneapolis: Abdo Publishing, 2017.


## NOTE TO EDUCATORS

Visit **www.focusreaders.com** to find lesson plans, activities, links, and other resources related to this title.

# INDEX



**Answer Key: 1.** Answers will vary; **2.** Answers will vary; **3.** A; **4.** B